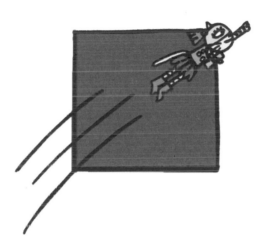

Fashion Kitty

AND THE Unlikely Hero

by Charise Mericle Harper

Disney · Hyperion Books
New York

Text and illustrations copyright © 2008
by Charise Mericle Harper
All rights reserved. Published by Disney · Hyperion Books, an imprint of Disney Book Group. No part of this book may be reproduced or transmitted in any form or by any means, electronic or mechanical, including photocopying, recording, or by any information storage and retrieval system, without written permission from the publisher.
For information address Disney · Hyperion Books,
114 Fifth Avenue, New York, New York 10011-5690.
Printed in Singapore
First Disney · Hyperion paperback edition, 2008
10 9 8 7 6 5 4 3 2
F850-6835-5-09349

Library of Congress Cataloging-in-Publication Data on file
Library of Congress Control Number: 2007938578
ISBN 978-0-7868-3727-4
Reinforced binding
Visit www.hyperionbooksforchildren.com

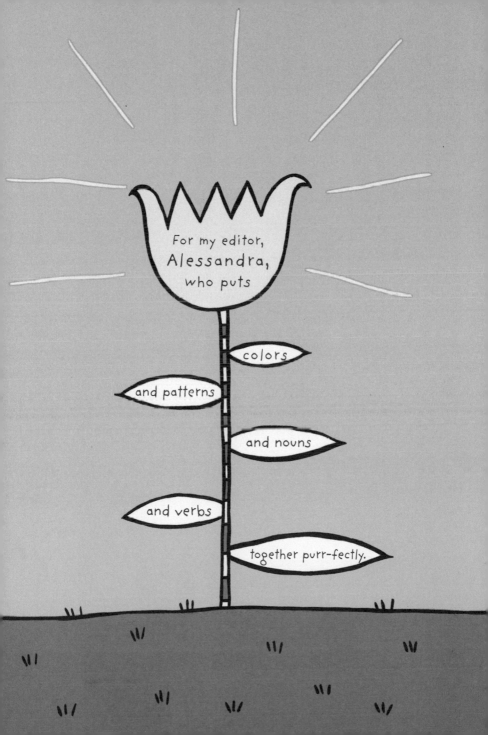

For my editor,
Alessandra,
who puts

colors

and patterns

and nouns

and verbs

together purr-fectly.

This is Kiki Kittie.

Kiki is not famous.

This is Fashion Kitty.

Fashion Kitty is famous.
Fashion Kitty is the secret superhero
identity of Kiki Kittie.

When you are famous you sometimes get your name in the newspaper.

This does not make everyone happy.

Kiki is not always patient with her little sister, Lana.

Mother Kittie, on the other hand, is always patient.

Lana was not the only one who was unhappy about Fashion Kitty's fame.

Mrs. Rumple sounded like a Fashion Kitty enemy.

Fashion is a waste of time.

How can I stop this fashion nonsense?

But that was only because she was the principal of Kiki Kittie's school.

It is my duty to make sure my students study and learn.

OATH OF PRINCIPALNESS

And she took her job very seriously.

If you were to ask the parents at the school, most would say . . .

Mrs. Rumple was good at her job because she was astute. This means she often noticed things, and sometimes guessed what was going to happen before it even happened.

For example, there was the time Morgan Maltese brought a superbouncy ball to school.

Minutes later . . .

Mrs. Rumple was right about the ball.

And Mrs. Rumple was right about the next day at school, too.

But being 100 percent
right did not make Mrs.
Rumple feel any better.

All the students had one main
subject on their kitty brains . . .

What would
I say to
Fashion Kitty
if I met her?

Where is
Fashion Kitty
going to
appear
next?

What does
Fashion Kitty
say about
fashion?

What
can
Fashion Kitty
do?

What does
Fashion Kitty
look like
when she
is
flying?

What would
Fashion Kitty
Think of
my outfit today?

Who has seen
Fashion
kitty?

Little piece for
everything else

and this left very little room
for regular school learning.

It was more than Mrs. Rumple could stand.

Something must be done immediately!

Mrs. Pettibottom, schedule a meeting with all the parents for tonight.

Mrs. Pettibottom was the school secretary.

Ooooohh! An emergency meeting. That sounds exciting.

Right away, Mrs. Rumple.

Mrs. Pettibottom liked Fashion Kitty, but it was something she tried to keep to herself.

She knew that any talk of Fashion Kitty put Mrs. Rumple into a bad mood, but sometimes she just couldn't help herself.

Grrr. Shouldn't you be getting to work?

Oops . . . I shouldn't have said anything.

Is this meeting about Fashion Kitty?

Yes, right away.

Mrs. Pettibottom got right to work.

Yes, a meeting tonight.

Seven p.m. in the school auditorium.

It's an emergency!

Meanwhile, Kiki and her classmates were
having a wonderful fashion-filled time.

Zack was a new boy friend for both Kiki and June.

And that's pretty much all they would say about it.

When Kiki, June, and Zack arrived at Kiki's house, Mother Kittie was on the phone.

. . . Of course, Mrs. Pettibottom. We can be at the meeting.

Kiki's mom is a really good cook.

Mother Kittie always remembered to put Mousie in her clubhouse

Be safe, Mousie.

and spray cream-cheese air freshener around the house

PFFT

before Kiki got home from school, just in case she brought any friends home with her.

The kittie family were vegetarians, which means they didn't eat meat.

Of course, Mousie* was very happy about this.

*Also known as: Phoebe Frederique

Usually, even Lana was pretty careful not to mention Mousie. But sometimes she forgot.

That night, Mother and Father Kittie and almost two hundred other kitty parents filed into the school auditorium for the big meeting.

At the end of the meeting,
Mrs. Rumple was very happy. . . .

But Mrs. Rumple was wrong about the everyone-being-happier part.

Kiki is going to be upset.

I know.

Why are you looking so sad? Did something bad happen?

Something horrible and awful and terrible happened!

What! What's going on? Tell me!

And then Father Kittie tried to tell Kiki all about the meeting.

Let's see . . . there were lots of parents there.

We met your friend Jack's mother.

Zack! Not Jack.

And then Mother Kittie interrupted.

The next morning it took kiki less than three
minutes to get dressed for school. There was

no organizing,

no deciding,

and no modeling in front of the mirror.

When you don't have any choices,
it doesn't take long to put . . .

this outfit   on   this body.

white shirt

Blue
skirt

white socks

I
HATE
YOU!

Kiki was grumpy,

grumpy,

and even more grumpy.

But then Lana came into the kitchen.

Look, Kiki, I'm wearing a uniform, like you.

2 shirts

2 skirts

Socks →

Oh, Lana.

After Kiki left for school,

Bye, Kiki, have a nice day.

Bye.

Mother Kittie gave Lana an extra hug.

Thank you, Lana.

You're welcome.

What did I do?

Kiki noticed two new things on the way to school.

Kiki didn't want anyone to think Fashion Kitty was uncaring. Kiki wanted to say . . .

But she didn't say that, because in her very own heart she felt exactly the same as the other kitties.

And, while Mrs. Rumple was right about the studying part . . .

. . . she was wrong about the fashion part. For example, the students still found time to complain about the uniforms.

Even some of the boys complained.

That night, Kiki tried to accessorize her look to make the uniform look less dreadful.

The only things she could change were her hair ribbons and her shoes, and that wasn't very exciting.

For the next few days everyone went a little shoe-crazy...

These boots don't go, but I don't care. Nothing goes with this dumb uniform.

Did you see that kitty wearing flip-flops?

Huh?

... even Mother Kittie.

Here's a feel-better present, Kiki.

Oh, thank you! Red cowboy boots. I love them so much.

There are two types of kitties:

and kiki was definitely a saver.

Even though shoes are fun and great to look at, you can only talk about shoes so much. . . .

But just because Mrs. Rumple couldn't hear fashion talking, it didn't mean there wasn't fashion talking going on.

And so was invented the Fabulous Feline Fashion Flyer.

Since everyone was starved for fashion talk, the flyer was an instant success,

even among the teachers.

But surprisingly, nothing did.

... FASHION KITTY!

Fashion Kitty landed on the balcony outside Becky Burmese's window.

Fashion Kitty breathed a frustrated sigh and said . . .

Fashion Kitty was astounded, astonished, and shocked. She couldn't think of a single thing to say.

And with that, Becky Burmese walked out of her bedroom and shut the door.

Fashion Kitty had a very confused flight home.

When Kiki walked in the door, Lana was in bed, and Mother and Father Kittie were watching TV. Kiki was glad to have the kitchen all to herself.

But Kiki was wrong. The next day was even more confusing.

Oh, my gosh! It's the flip-flop kitty...

...and she's wearing socks and flip-flops!

Hi, Kiki.

What are you looking at?

That kitty with the socks and flip-flops?

That's Becky.

Why is she wearing flip-flops?

Nothing interesting happened the rest of the day, and this was a very unusual thing after a Fashion Kitty visit.

That is, until Zack showed up.

On the walk home, Kiki found out four new things about Zack:

 Zack had a pet goldfish, which was an unusual pet for a cat to have.

 Zack did not have any brothers or sisters.

Zack did not like the new uniforms. Most of the boys didn't seem to care so much one way or the other.

MOST BOYS

It's a shirt and pants. Big deal.

ZACK

The shirt is too tight.

And the pants aren't comfy.

 Zack loved cheese.

I just made some tasty cheese biscuits. Who wants one?

Hmmm. Interesting.

Can I have one? Cheese is my favorite.

It's hard to be sad about your life and keep two big secrets all at the same time.

I wish I could tell someone about Fashion Kitty.

Do you like cheese, too?

Squeak, squeak. That's Mousie talk for "yes."

I wonder if I could tell Zack about Mousie. He does have a pet goldfish.

Lana, stop it!

It's okay, she's not bugging me.

Squeak, squeak, squeak, squeak, squeak, squeak.

You're being annoying!

After Zack left, Lana said . . .

The next morning Kiki felt a little better.
Sometimes a sunny day can do that.

Hi, Kiki, how are you?

Good.

Do you want to see the new flyer I made last night?

You bet.

Oh, June, it's great! You are so dedicated.

Thanks.

FLIP FLOP

FLIP FLOP

Kiki wanted to tell her best friend all about Becky and what she had said when Fashion Kitty tried to help her. But how could she do that and keep her Fashion Kitty identity a secret? It was impossible!

It was another ordinary day, until Zack shared some spying news.

June avoided Kiki the next morning.
This is not an unusual thing to do
when you are angry with someone,
and it can be quite effective if you
want to hurt their feelings.

I haven't seen June today.

I guess she's still mad.

When a principal asks you to do something, you mostly have to do it, whether you want to do it or not.

Kiki had two guesses about tomorrow:

ONE   TWO

Kiki didn't want to make June angry, but the Becky mystery was too hard for her to ignore. She couldn't help it. She couldn't even wait for Zack.

I need to know what Becky is doing.

The next day, both of Kiki's guesses came true. First, number two, and then, number one.

No help again today! I can't believe you!

Kiki could hardly wait to tell Zack all about it.

Later that day, Mrs. Rumple organized a school assembly, and what she had to say surprised and shocked everybody, especially Kiki.

Kiki didn't know what to do, and now there were two kitties who were angry at her.

It was not a good feeling.

Sometimes, when things are going poorly,
a kitty might think . . .

But this doesn't help for long if the kitty is
wrong, and this time Kiki was very wrong.

Mrs. Rumple's office was not anyone's favorite place to go, except for maybe Mrs. Rumple.

Someone told me that you two have been lurking around in the hallway outside my office.

Who said that? Did Becky say that?

Because we are pretty sure that Becky is the one who is putting the gum on your chair. She's sneaky!

We've seen her outside your office a lot!

Zack, we can't say for sure she did anything wrong!

Yes, we can! She did it! She's guilty!

Kiki spent the rest of the afternoon feeling sad, alone, and very guilty about getting Becky into trouble.

And even though she didn't say anything to June, Kiki made one more promise.

I'm not going to spy on Becky anymore.

Little did Kiki know that this was not going to be a hard promise to keep.

Then, quick as a flash . . .

It's Fashion Kitty to the rescue!

The signal was not hard to find.

It was hard to say who was more surprised.

Luckily, Fashion Kitty could fly, so she was not injured when she fell. Mrs. Rumple was not so lucky.

And for the first time ever, Fashion Kitty and
Mrs. Rumple were thinking the exact same thing.

Thankfully, Mrs. Rumple was nothing like Becky.

Fashion Kitty wanted to help Mrs. Rumple, but she couldn't stop looking at the paper dolls hanging on the wall.

Mrs. Rumple took a deep breath, then told Fashion Kitty all about the paper dolls. There was a lot to tell.

Oh, yes, she's a very sweet kitty. A little annoying, but very thoughtful and caring.

It's hard for an old kitty like me to change her ways. I'm used to my dark blue suits.

She wants to try more adventurous clothes. Things like stripes or patterns, and colors that are not blue.

Every couple of days she slips one of these little paper dolls under my door to show me how I would look wearing something new.

Then she flip-flops in front of my door to let me know she's thinking of me.

Fashion Kitty couldn't think of what
to say next. Her kitty brain was
working overtime, which means superfast.

Then, suddenly, she was full of questions.

Mrs. Rumple was very organized. After all, she was a principal. She answered all of Fashion Kitty's questions in perfect order.

Over the next hour, Fashion Kitty persuaded Mrs. Rumple to try on a few new outfits.

Not surprisingly, all of Mrs. Rumple's new clothes were various shades of blue. They weren't very adventurous, but to Mrs. Rumple it was like the difference between walking on flat ground and climbing a mountain.

Not everyone can be adventurous on their own. Sometimes a kitty needs a little help. And for the second time that day, the two kitties were thinking the exact same thing again.

Flying home, Fashion Kitty did a lot of thinking about being brave.

It is definitely harder to be a brave kitty when no one knows you are being brave.

By the time she walked into her house, she had it all figured out in her head. As always, her family was happy to see her.

Good. You're home safe.

Yeah! Did you rescue someone?

I can't stay.

This time someone else is the fashion hero.

Within minutes, Fashion Kitty was flying again.

Epilogue

Yes, this is the end
of this part of the
story. Here is what
happened next—
because it's always
nice to know how
everything turned out.
Isn't it?

The next school day was filled with surprises. Mrs. Rumple wore something that was not a dark blue suit . . .

. . . and shared a secret with Mrs. Pettibottom.

Becky, sans flip-flops, wore a bright red pair of brand-new cowboy boots.

Kiki had a new idea for the Fashion Flyer.

Zack apologized to Kiki and shared some gossip he had heard.

This was especially exciting for June.

And someone, quietly and discreetly,
which means without anyone noticing,
threw away two packages of gum.

FASHION Kitty's

FABULOUS

Handy Fashion Help

FUN

Dress up Kiki and June

PAGES

Are you having a fashion emergency?

WHY NOT TRY FASHION KITTY'S
Mini FASHION HELPER?

HERE'S ① Start with a normal piece of paper.

How to make it.

② Now you need to make a square. Fold corner over to edge.

③ Cut this rectangle off.

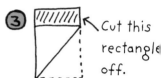

④ Open square and fold the other way.

FOLD 2

FOLD 1

⑤ Fold all 4 corners to meet at center point.

FIRST FOLDOVER

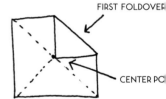

CENTER PO

⑥ Now your folded paper looks like this.

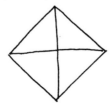

⑦ Turn your paper over and fold all 4 corners to center again.

8 FOLD IN HALF

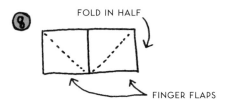

FINGER FLAPS

9 Put fingers and thumbs in flaps and push toward center.

THIS IS A VIEW FROM THE TOP.

10 Now open it all up and add colors and fashion tips like this one, or enlarge this one on a photocopier and fold it up.

MORE →

PAGE O' TOPS

TABS TO FOLD BACK ↑

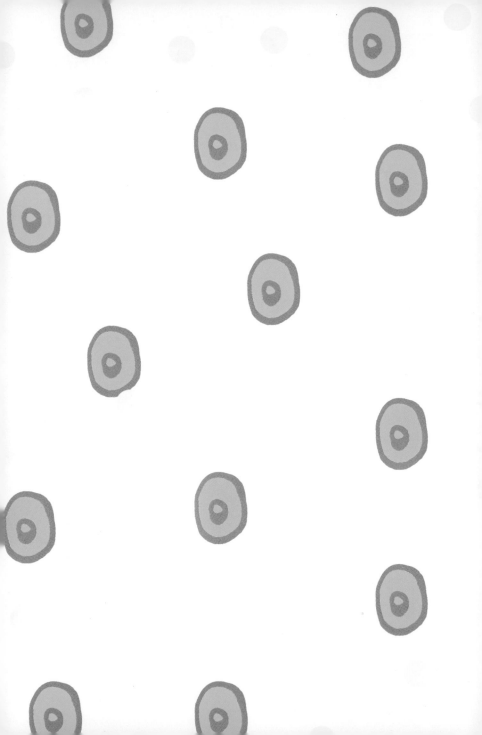

PAGE O' BOTTOMS

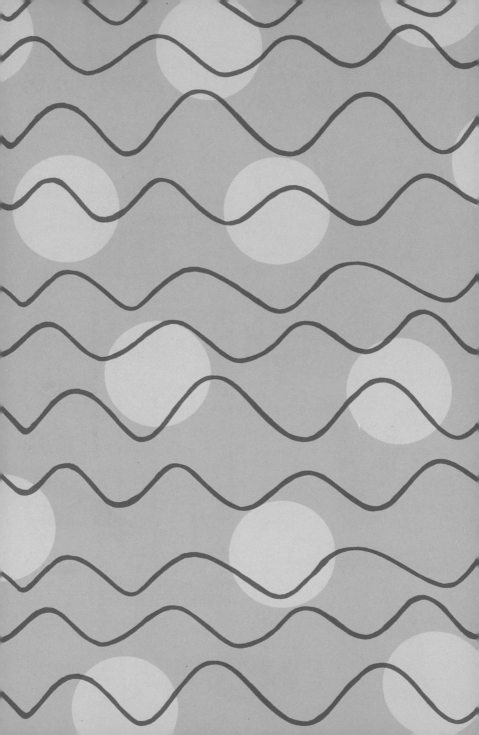

DRAW FASHION KITTY

①

START WITH AN OVAL.

②

ADD 2 SMALL CIRCLES.

③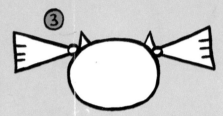

ADD TRIANGLES ON EACH SIDE
FOR HAIR AND ON TOP FOR EARS.

④

DRAW LINE LOWER THAN
HALFWAY DOWN.

⑤

ADD 2 EYES AND EYELASHES.

⑥

ADD A TRIANGLE NOSE.

⑦

DRAW A MOUTH, FRECKLES,
AND WHISKERS.

Thank you for
drawing me!